This Is the Da[illegible]

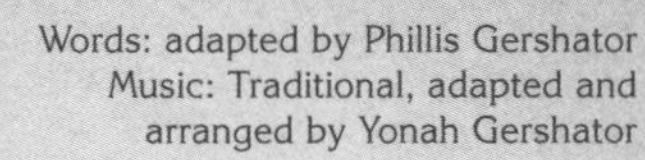

Words: adapted by Phillis Gershator
Music: Traditional, adapted and arranged by Yonah Gershator

Moderate, not too fast

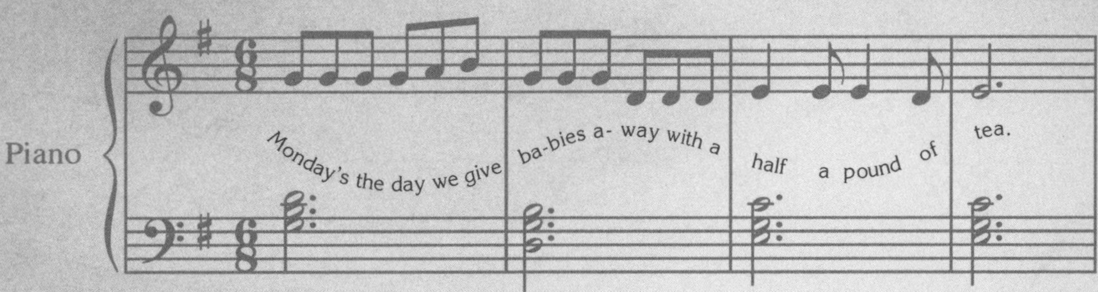
Piano
Monday's the day we give ba-bies a- way with a half a pound of tea.

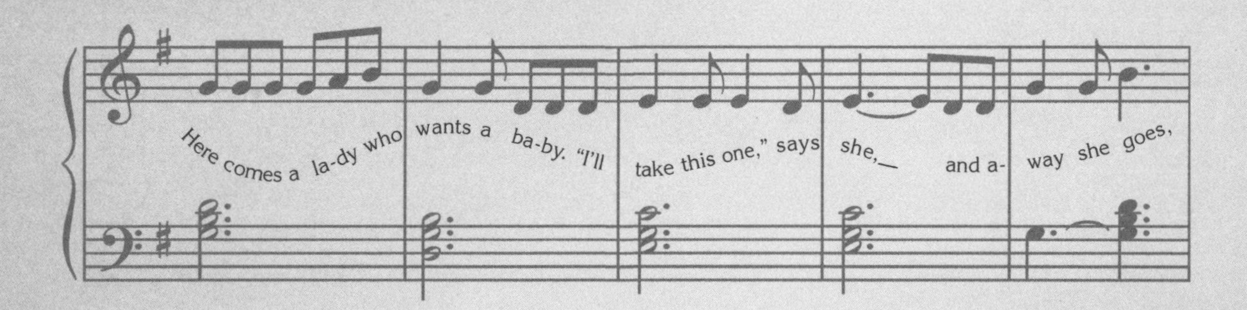
Here comes a la-dy who wants a ba-by. "I'll take this one," says she,_ and a- way she goes,

kiss-ing its toes. Tra la and fid-dle de dee.__ And a- way she goes kiss-ing its toes.

Tra la and fid-dle de dee!

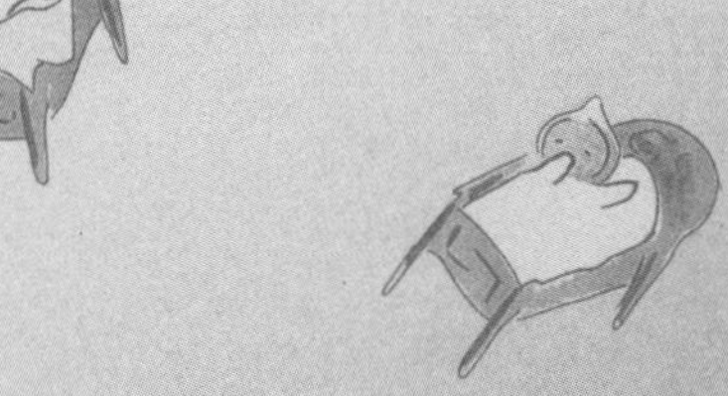

This Is the Day!
Adapted by Phillis Gershator
Illustrated by Marjorie Priceman
Houghton Mifflin Company • Boston 2007

Monday's the day we give babies away
with a half a pound of tea.

Here comes a lady who wants a baby.
"I'll take this one," says she,

TEA
TEA

and away she goes, kissing its toes.
Tra la and fiddle de dee.

Tuesday's the day we give babies away
with milk and cookies for free.

A lady says, "Ooh, I will gladly take two.
It's double the fun," says she.

"My own girl and boy!" she cries for joy.
Tra la and fiddle de dee.

Wednesday's the day we give babies away
with a bear and a honeybee.
From a hot air balloon, a sweet lady croons,
"I have plenty of room for three."

Higher she flies, singing lullabies.
Tra la and fiddle de dee.

Thursday's the day we give babies away
with a cradle on top of a tree.
The lady at the door chooses two and two more.
"The four that can snore," says she.

Then she's off with a hop to meet the new pop.
Tra la and fiddle de dee.

Friday's the day we give babies away
with a barrel of fish from the sea.

One lady can't wait. She speeds through the gate.
"I'll take these five," says she.

Each little tyke has a seat on her bike.
Tra la and fiddle de dee.

Saturday's the day we give babies away
with a happiness guarantee.

A lady has fun picking more than one.
"Six is a good mix," says she.

With three on each hip, she sails off on a ship.
Tra la and fiddle de dee.

Sunday's the day we give babies away.
A lady shouts, "Save some for me!"

She rides in from the west
and chooses the rest.

"Seven is heaven," says she.

All of the ladies love all of the babies.
What a sight to see!

Calloo, Callay for Baby Day!
Tra la and fiddle de dee.

A Note from the Author

I first heard "This Is the Day We Give Babies Away" in the 1960s, and given its catchy tune and unusual lyrics, the song stuck with me for all these years. After expanding it into a tale of happy adoptions, I learned more about the song's origins, thanks to Mark D. Moss of *Sing Out!* and Joe "The Songfinder" Hickerson.

Since the beginning of the 1900s, and possibly before, "This Is the Day" was sung in various parts of the United States. It may have originally come to these shores from England. Sung by folks in the Ozarks, westerners, and soldiers during World War II, it was recorded first by singer Rosalie Sorrels in *Rosalie's Songbag* and more recently in her 1990 release, *Be Careful, There's a Baby in the House.* On *Be Careful,* Rosalie Sorrels sings her own humorous version, written with Olive Wooly Burt, titled "The Baby Tree."

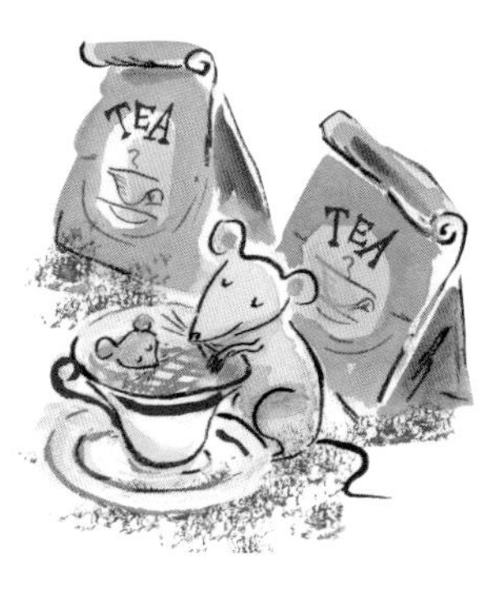
TEA
TEA

Text and sheet music adapted and arranged from a traditional song.

www.houghtonmifflinbooks.com

The text of this book is set in Korinna.
The illustrations are watercolor.

Library of Congress Cataloging-in-Publication Data
Gershator, Phillis.
This is the day! / adapted by Phillis Gershator from a traditional song;
illustrated by Marjorie Priceman.
p. cm.
Summary: Presents an expanded version of a folk song in which
babies are happily adopted on each day of the week.
ISBN 0-618-49746-3 (hardcover)
1. Folk songs, English—United States—Texts. [1. Babies—Songs and music. 2. Counting—
Songs and music. 3. Folk songs—United States.] I. Priceman, Marjorie, ill. II. Title.
PZ8.3.G3235Th 2006 782.42—dc22 [E] 2005004258

ISBN-13: 978-0618-49746-1

Printed in Singapore
TWP 10 9 8 7 6 5 4 3 2 1

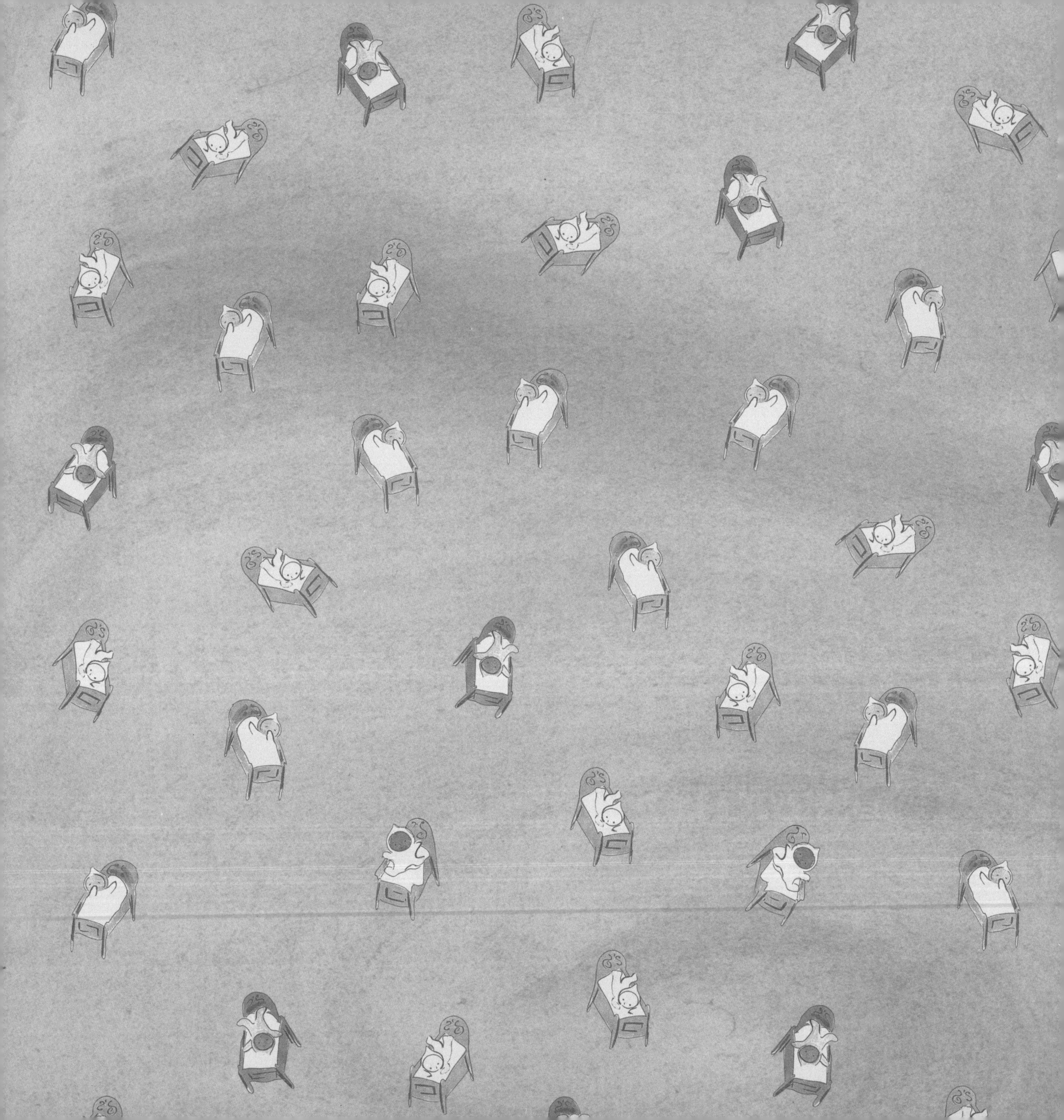